Richard Scarry's
Best Friend Ever

GW00992133

A GOLDEN BOOK • NEW YORK
Western Publishing Company, Inc., Racine, Wisconsin 53404

©1989 Richard Scarry. All rights reserved. Printed in Italy. No part of this book may be reproduced or copied in any form without written permission from the publisher. All trademarks are the property of Western Publishing Company, Inc. Library of Congress Catalog Card Number: 88-51408 ISBN: 0-307-11715-4/ISBN: 0-307-61715-7 (lib. bdg.)   MCMXCII

Pickles Pig and his family moved to a new house. Pickles had his very own room, which he liked very much. It was bigger and nicer than his old room.

There was a big garage, too.
Pickles could park his toy car
right next to his father's car.

Pickles liked the woods near his house.
He loved to climb the trees and play on
the swing his father made for him.

There was a park nearby, too. Pickles enjoyed going there and sailing his little boat on the pond.

Pickles also liked his new neighbours. Still, Pickles was a little sad because there wasn't anyone in the neighbourhood who was is age. If only he had a friend to play with and share the fun.

One day Pickles heard loud noises
coming from the vacant lot across the
street. He saw a big digger making
a large hole in the ground.

A little bunny and his father stood on
the pavement, watching the big machine.
The little bunny was the same age
as Pickles.

Pickles asked his mother to take him across
the street to meet the little bunny.

"My name is Wiggles. My father is having a new house built for our family to live in. That digger is digging out the cellar," the little bunny said.

"I'm Pickles," said Pickles Pig. "I'm so glad that we will be neighbours. Ever since I moved here I've wanted a friend I could play with."

Each day Pickles looked
at the vacant site. One day
a bricklayer came to build
the foundation of Wiggles's
new house.

Carpenters came and built
the floors, the walls,
and the roof.

Then the carpenters put in the windows
and a door.

Soon the plumbers
and the electricians
came to do their work.

A few days later the painters arrived and
began painting the house. A gardener planted
flowers and bushes around the house. The house
was just about finished. Soon it would be ready
for Pickles's new friend and his family.

At last the happy day arrived. Pickles
was so excited when he saw the moving van
stop in front of the new house.

Soon after, the Bunny family drove up in their car.

"Hi, Pickles. We're here at last," Wiggles shouted.

From that day on, Pickles and Wiggles were the best of friends. They had fun playing on the swing in the woods and climbing trees.

They went to the park
and sailed Pickles's little
boat on the pond.

They had fun
playing tag,

leapfrog, and all
kinds of games.

They drove down the street together,
Pickles in his car and Wiggles on his
tricycle. They waved to all their neighbours.

"This is my best friend, Wiggles,"
Pickles told them.

Pickles was very happy to have a friend like Wiggles. They shared their toys and went everywhere together.

"You're the best friend ever," Pickles told Wiggles.

"And so are you," replied Wiggles.